W9-BRG-836

The Best Valentine In The World

E.G. Sherburne School

by Marjorie Weinman Sharmat

illustrated by Lilian Obligado

Holiday House

NEW YORK

Library of Congress Cataloging in Publication Data

Sharmat, Marjorie Weinman.
The best valentine in the world.

SUMMARY: Although Ferdinand has worked on his
valentine for Florette since November, he's sure
that she's forgotten him on Valentine's Day.
[1. Valentines—Fiction. 2. Foxes—Fiction.
3. Valentine's Day—Fiction] I. Obligado, Lilian,
ill. II. Title.
PZ7.S5299Be   [E]   81-13345
ISBN 0-8234-0440-4   AACR2

To my valentines,
N.W. *and* A.R.,
November 5, 1922

It was NOVEMBER 5TH.

Ferdinand Fox was looking forward to Valentine's Day. "Only one hundred more days," he thought. "Only one hundred days until Florette Fox gives me a valentine." Ferdinand looked at his calendar. "I'd better start making *her* valentine now."

Ferdinand got crayons and paste and scissors, ribbons, lace and flowers, and purple paper. "Everyone gives red valentines," he thought, "so I'm going to make Florette something different. A purple valentine."

Ferdinand worked on his valentine all through November 5th, 6th, 7th and 8th. Then he looked it over. "This valentine doesn't quite meet my high standards," he decided. "I need more things to put on it."

Ferdinand went outside and walked through the woods. He gathered some leaves. "I will paste these on my valentine for a nice leafy look," he thought. Then he saw a couple of flowers.

"November flowers," he said. "If they lasted this long, maybe they will hold up through February!" Ferdinand picked the flowers. He kept walking and looking. "Sticks!" he exclaimed. "I could spell out Florette's name with sticks." Ferdinand picked up the sticks.

Then Ferdinand went back inside. He worked on his valentine through the rest of November and all through December. "What a masterpiece! This is the best valentine in the world!" he said as he finished it in the middle of January. "But Florette deserves this. Because I know she's making *me* a valentine at this very moment. Not as great as the one I made for her, of course, but it's the thought that counts."

• February 1982 •

Sunday		7	14	21	28
monday	1	8	15	22
Tuesday	2	9	16	23
Wednesday	3	10	17	24
Thursday	4	11	18	25
Friday	5	12	19	26
Saturday	6	13	20	27

Ferdinand telephoned Florette. "What have you been doing lately?" he asked.

"Nothing special," said Florette.

"Nothing special!" thought Ferdinand. "She doesn't want to tell me about the valentine she's making for me. She's working away into the night, she hasn't combed her fur in weeks, she hasn't read any good books, hasn't seen a movie, all because of me. Florette really cares."

Finally it was February 14th. Ferdinand thought, "I'll go to Florette's house and let her give me my valentine first. Then I'll surprise her with mine."

Ferdinand searched for a bag big enough to hold his valentine. At last he found a garbage bag. "Florette will never guess that anything so wonderful is in something so plain."

Ferdinand went to Florette's house. "Happy Valentine's Day," he said.

"Oh, is it Valentine's Day?" asked Florette. "After Christmas, Hanukkah, and New Year's Day, I sort of poop out with holidays. I'm glad you reminded me, though."

"So what are you going to do about it?" asked Ferdinand.

"You sound mad," said Florette.

"I *am* mad," said Ferdinand. "You're celebrating Valentine's Day by forgetting about it."

Ferdinand turned to leave.

"What do you have in that bag?" asked Florette.

"In here? Oh, it's my garbage," said Ferdinand.

"Your garbage? Why did you bring it to my house?" asked Florette.

"I brought it to celebrate Valentine's Day, you forgetter, you!" said Ferdinand, and he marched off.

"*Garbage* for Valentine's Day?" said Florette, scratching her head. "That's a new one."

Ferdinand hurried home. "She *forgot*. What a terrible thing to do to February 14th."

At home, Ferdinand took his valentine out of the bag. "Now I'm the permanent owner of a masterpiece. A masterpiece that has FLORETTE written all over it."

Ferdinand's telephone rang.

"Hello, it's February 14th, Valentine's Day, spread the word," he answered.

"I know it. It's me, Florette," said Florette. "I have something for you."

"What?" asked Ferdinand.

"Something," said Florette. "Come and get it."

"It's a last-minute valentine, isn't it?" said Ferdinand. "It's just a couple of pieces of paper stuck together with paste running over the edges and with BE MY VALENTINE scribbled on it so fast that VALENTINE is probably misspelled, right?"

"V-A-L-E-N-T-I-N-E," Florette spelled. "Do you want it?"

"I'm thinking about it," said Ferdinand. "I bet the paste isn't even dry yet, is it?"

"It's dry. It's dry, and I'm getting mad," said Florette. "This valentine is what I would call beautiful, gorgeous, spectacular, just to name a few descriptions."

"Ha!" said Ferdinand.

"Ha yourself!" said Florette. And she hung up.

"What a sad way to celebrate Valentine's Day," thought Ferdinand. "It could have been a day of beauty and lace and sticks and purple paper.

Ferdinand kept thinking about Florette. "So she forgot," he said at last. "Not everyone has a fine memory like me. Not everyone is organized and clear-headed and thinking ahead." Ferdinand stared at his valentine. "I made this valentine just for Florette, and I'm going to give it to her."

Ferdinand took the valentine and went to Florette's house.
He held the valentine behind his back when Florette opened
the door.

"Happy Valentine's Day again," he said. Then he held the valentine in front of Florette's face. "A purple valentine, just for you."

"Oh, oh, oh," said Florette. "It's a masterpiece! Come in with your valentine."

Ferdinand stepped inside. "I knew you'd love it," he said. "And don't feel bad about your last-minute valentine. You don't even have to *give* it to me. You mean much more to me than any old valentine. Or any new, just-made, last-minute, paste-dripping-from-the-edges valentine."

"But," said Florette, "I made one for you, and I want to give it to you."

Florette opened her closet and dragged out a valentine that reached almost to the ceiling.

It was covered with ribbons and flowers and lace and stars and bits of velvet and satin, and sparkles and candy hearts with candy arrows, and feathers, and the words FERDINAND'S VALENTINE which had little bells that jingled. And it was green.

"Wow!" said Ferdinand. "It *is* beautiful, gorgeous, spectacular, just to name a few descriptions. You work fast."

"Slow," said Florette. "I made this last year between St. Patrick's Day and the Fourth of July. I wanted to be sure I had a wonderful valentine for you. Then I put it away and forgot about it. Until you reminded me today. I hope you like green valentines. Everyone gives red."

"It's the best valentine in the world," said Ferdinand, "and I feel stupid."

"Well, I feel forgetful," said Florette, "so let's call it even."

"Okay," said Ferdinand. "Happy Valentine's Day for the third time."

"And a happy Valentine's Day to you, too," said Florette.

FIC Sharmat, Marjorie Weinman
Sha   The Best Valentine in
          the World